I WILL!

A Book of Promises

BY JUANA MEDINA

Versify
Houghton Mifflin Harcourt
Boston   New York

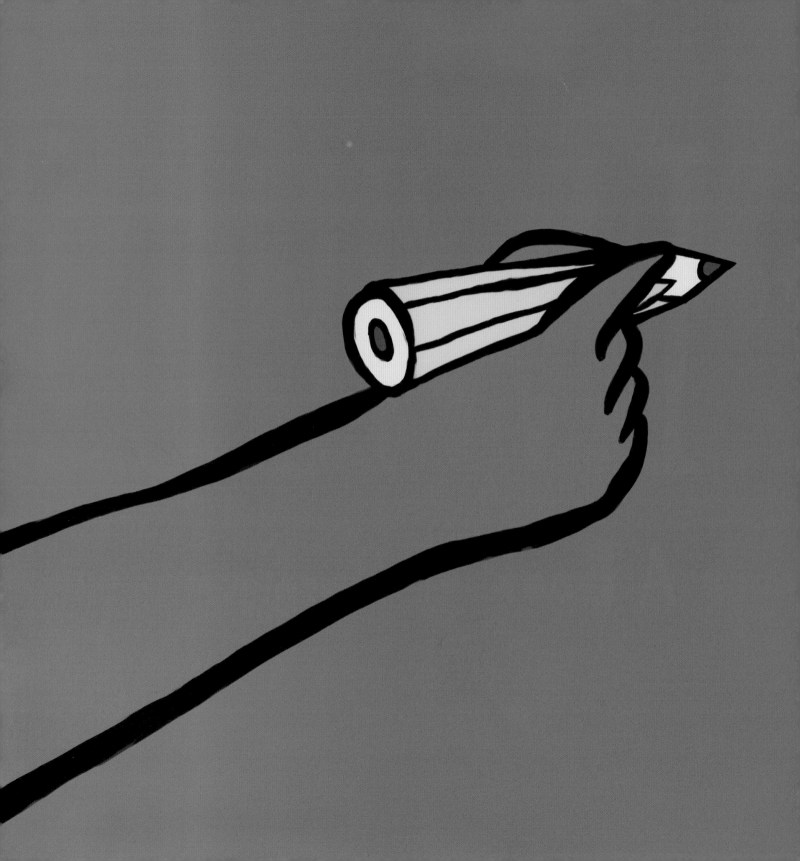

To Raya, whose will is powerful & magical ♡

All my gratitude to Margaret Raymo and Celeste Knudsen for their guidance and expertise.
Thanks, also, to Kwame Alexander for believing in this series.

The illustrations in this book were created digitally in Procreate (in the heart of the wee hours as my twin sons slept). The body text was hand lettered by Juana Medina.

The Library of Congress Cataloging-in-Publication Data is available.
ISBN: 978-0-358-55559-9

Manufactured in China
SCP 10 9 8 7 6 5 4 3 2 1
4500824171

I, _____
WRITE YOUR NAME HERE

will try to keep
this promise as
best as I can.

I will be
kind to
others.

I will be
kind to
myself.

I will tell the truth, even if it's hard.

I will learn!
I will explore!

I will

problem

solve!

I will help those in need

and ask for
help when
I need it.

I will rest
when I'm tired
and enjoy
the quiet.

I will
have
fun!

I will love myself.

I will
love
others.

I will love
and protect
nature.

I will
join with
you

to make
this a
better
world